Christmas at the Four Corners of the Earth

by

BLAISE CENDRARS

TRANSLATED BY BERTRAND MATHIEU
PEN & INK DRAWINGS BY DENZIL WALKER

*

BOA Editions, Ltd. ✳ Brockport, New York ✳ 1994

Noël aux quatre coins du monde originally published by
Editions Denoel, Paris, copyright © 1953
English translation copyright © 1994 by Bertrand Mathieu
Pen & Ink Drawings © 1994 by Denzil Walker
Manufactured in the United States of America

LC #: 94–71934
ISBN: 1–880238–16–0

First Edition
94 95 96 97 98 5 4 3 2 1

The publication of books by BOA Editions, Ltd., is made possible with the
assistance of grants from the Literature Program of the New York State
Council on the Arts and the Literature Program of the National
Endowment for the Arts, as well as from the Lannan Foundation,
the Lila Wallace–Reader's Digest Literary Publishers Marketing
Development Program, the Rochester Area Foundation,
and contributions from individual supporters.

Pen & Ink Drawings: Denzil Walker
Cover Design: Daphne Poulin
Typesetting: Richard Foerster
Manufacturing: McNaughton & Gunn
BOA Logo: Mirko

BOA Editions, Ltd.
A. Poulin, Jr., President
92 Park Avenue
Brockport, NY 14420

*This translation is dedicated to
my two grown American children,
Russell and Rachel,
and to my three small French children,
Michael, Nathaniel & Kenneth,
who all know, deep down, that
Christmas and this earth
aren't necessarily incompatible*

"*When are we going to take off, past the shores and the mountains, to greet the new task, the new wisdom, the defeat of tyrants and devils, the end of superstition—to worship*—the first to do so!—*Christmas on this earth?*"

—*Arthur Rimbaud*

Contents

Christmas
at the Four Corners of the Earth

Christmas in New Zealand

For Francine de Bovil

To the ends of the earth. Austral summer. It's Christmas. I've come ashore and from the top of the sand dune I can see a beach overflowing with people, city folk living it up behind the barriers that keep out the sharks. The whale-shark has three rows of teeth and six thousand teeth in each of its jaws. Yesterday, it was a flock of seals stretched out in the sun and, the day before, two pairs of walruses playing off shore. I tie up my horse and go down for a swim; then I come out, get dressed, leap in the saddle, do a quick turnabout, and make a beeline inland. It's Christmas. The shepherds. The star. The manger in Bethlehem. The crib. The blue angels of Piombino in the sacristy of the Vatican. The music of the spheres. *Peace on Earth, Good Will to Men....* The sheep. The other year, I was in Rome....

If anywhere on earth there exists a land of The Heart's Desire,[1] that place at a glance is New Zealand. On these two isles of the blessed, huge flocks of choice animals graze on the thick grass of the valleys. From one end of the year to the other, nothing comes to trouble them. You can travel by car for days or by horse for weeks without ever meeting a living soul. You can climb high ridges, go down into untracked valley depths without ever coming out of pastureland. Except for a petrified cataract, a shy little corner furnished in Swiss miniature and reserved for young newlyweds looking for a place to honeymoon or for old couples who want to celebrate their golden anniversary, a few groves of tropical plants—strange, rare, and as long-lived as those in Ceylon, especially the gigantic crucifix-shaped ferns which are all that's left of the primitive flora of the countryside—nothing picturesque assaults the eye. The whole interior of the country is divided into rectangles by high fences of five-layered barbed wire separating the grazing areas; whole valleys casually box in other valleys; hillsides are followed by hillsides; nothing seems to want to disturb the uniformity, the monotony of glittering grass spread out everywhere, this grass of somber green which reflects the sky like water, which engulfs the countryside and gives it an appearance of quiet, of rest, of peace, of warm silence.

By chance and with a little luck, you can come upon a cluster of large eucalyptus trees which—under their sweet-smelling shadows, full of the cooing of turtledoves and the shivering of cardboard leaves—shelter a farm, if you can call a farm this freshly-built bungalow where a settler who is not a "peasant" and his lady who is not a "farmer's wife" sit down at night before their player piano or hunch over their portable radio.

Night was coming, Christmas night. I'd been out trotting all day and I'd gotten completely lost. And I continued trotting a long time in this night riddled with stars, disoriented, not so much by the stunning brightness of the Southern Cross[2] as by the millions of blinking lights from the bewildering fireflies....

Finally, I dismounted in a little wood. I tied my horse to a tree. The eucalyptus trees smelled so good. A faint light came through the trunks and some music as well. A piano. Someone's home was planted here at the mouth of a valley.

I approached it without making a sound and in my mind's eye I still have the picture of a pretty unbelievable sight: a man and a woman, he in a tuxedo, she in a *décolleté* evening gown, with a string of pearls around her neck. They sat side by side on an upholstered stool and played the piano with *three* hands, their backs turned to the open window. It was *Pagliacci.*[3] Behind them, on a table, an oil lamp, a plum pudding in a tinware water-bath on a spirit-stove, a bottle of whiskey, some glasses.... I stood there a long while, despite the fatigue that weighed me down, looking at those two people serenading each other, shoulder to shoulder, smiling brightly. They were alone on the face of the Earth....

At midnight, I introduced myself to them. They didn't tell me their story. Maybe they didn't have one. They were a happy couple and had chosen to be so in solitude. It's a priceless secret.... Peace.... Happiness.... But no one goes through his whole life in such *total* isolation, and the man had been in the war and, like me, he'd left an arm there....

Strange encounter. But that Christmas night was a good one. He with the right, I with the left. We guzzled.

An Anzac from Artois.[4]

My God, how small the world is when you travel...!

圖羊斬豬射
霧斬羊閒菌

萬前非妹月有妖秦

萬前非妹月有妖秦畫

Christmas
and New Year's Day in China

For Raymone

C hristmas in the North of China, 1929. I had an oppor-
tunity to compare the little terra-cotta figurines of
Marseilles or the mangers of Saint-Rémy-de-Provence
with what I had right there before my eyes, a manger built in
mid-air, a manger in the snow, a manger made up of real
people, real but not alive.

The troops of General Ma⁵ have sacked the premises of a
Catholic mission and massacred the Fathers and the livestock.
The troops of General Ma know the Christian calendar and
they know it's Christmas. So, in order to mock the converted
Chinese, they've built a manger on a hillside not far from the
village.

If you want to imagine the scene, you've got to think of the
title of the novel by Jules Janin,⁶ *The Dead Donkey and the
Guillotined Woman.* The donkey's dead, all right, but they've

managed to raise the carcass upright next to the carcass of a buffalo. All the other personages have been put in place with an almost devout care: the Child Jesus is a disemboweled baby boy, the Three Kings are offering their guts and their severed limbs, and the Blessed Virgin carries her head in her apron. *Voilà*, a manger *à la chinoise.* In the foreground, General Ma's soldiers march past and look with intense curiosity, as if they expected the tableau to come alive. The troops disappear in a turbulence of snow....

In 1930, General Ma, who was still plundering the province of Jo-Ho, came back to the same region with his troops. The earth was yellowish, the peasants were working in the fields, and, according to the Chinese calendar, it was their New Year's Day. The general ordered all the workers put to the sword, and to mock the inhabitants of the village, he invited them to come and visit a boxing ring that he'd ordered built on the same hill, but on the opposite side, a ring unique of its kind where the beheaded, held upright by stakes driven in the ground, faced each other like boxers and menaced each other with sawed-off fists. It was the very same general and the same soldiers, but they had changed sides and now belonged to the opposite army. The show was free and given for propaganda purposes. Should I call such propaganda "forward-looking"...? Or what...?

A dozen heads were scattered on the ground or suspended by their braids from the roosts the whole length of the spectators' enclosure.

Christmas with Max Jacob

For Nino and Simone Frank

This took place around 1921, and Max Jacob[7] was still living on the rue Gabrielle.[8] He'd told me to meet him at the Church of the Abbesses for the midnight mass and, sure enough, I'd spotted him arriving a bit ahead of time.

He'd dressed up to the hilt—opera hat, frock coat, cravat, monocle, shined shoes, overcoat buttoned up to the chin to conceal his lack of underclothes. He had his little rug under his arm, which he unrolled right away, to kneel down on. But since he'd begun to suffer from rheumatism, he found it quite uncomfortable to kneel down; so much so that, as soon as he'd knelt down, he stood up again without missing even a minute of the rite of the mass.... He rolled up, in order to change places. He moved elsewhere, with me right behind him. After changing to another altar, it turned out he couldn't hear well, so he came back to his first place. All this with polite bows, smiles, and a thousand *sotto-voce* excuses, interrupting, whenever necessary, his prayer or his hymn. The people knew him,

they were used to him. Then, after three or four displacements, he whispered to me: "Decidedly, I much prefer Sacré-Coeur. I feel infinitely more at home there...."

And he skipped out. I barely had time to see him taking the steps four at a time, he was already so far away, climbing toward the summit of the Mount, his rug rolled under his arm, rushing along because he didn't want to miss the end of the ceremony....

I'm quite sure that was one of the last times I saw Max.

Christmas
with the Indians of New Mexico

For Raymond and Gaby Manevy

A mong the Redskins of New Mexico, the place of the Christmas tree is taken by a multicolored rainbow made of tissue paper placed over two chairs above a peat fire that's kept burning all night long and whose warm air inflates the tissue rainbow like a hot air balloon, and I was expecting—just like in Naples on the feast of Piedigrotta when they launch the tissue balloons gifted with such marvelous powers of ascent due to the hot air emitted by a cotton-wool pad dipped in alcohol which the improvised airship carries at its base and which they light at the moment of launching so that the night is fully illuminated with transparent globes which soar at different heights and often catch fire—I was expecting at any moment to see the rainbow, inflated to the bursting point, slip its moorings and take off and vanish into thin air. But nothing of the sort....

Crouching around the fire, rapt in meditation before their multicolored rainbow, hypnotized, the Indians ruminate without saying a word, chewing their drug, a small sacred cactus no bigger than a mushroom, the famous peyote, the plant that fills the eyes with wonders.

Whole hours pass....

Are they dreaming?

The past?

The future?

We know they feel exiled in their own country....

And all of a sudden there's the rush. It's a dignified craziness. As if impelled by who-knows-what ancient fury, they all stand up together and go bounding out of the communal house.

Twenty-five years ago, they used to jump on their horses on Christmas night and give themselves over to an insane race on the only road of the pueblo, and the women bombarded them with watermelons to get the horses excited and see them take off at full speed in a cloud of dust. Nowadays, they jump into their cars and all go racing like bats out of hell to the state-line where they regroup, bumper to bumper, and lapse into meditation....

On the other side, there's a mushroom-city surrounded by oil wells. Illuminated billboards on the roofs, searchlights, neon signs, shrill loudspeakers. Through the open doors of night clubs comes dance music, followed by the lurching lyrics of romance and songs that have firewater on their breath....

The Indian who crosses the line illegally doesn't come back.

The place is called Stinking Springs, or Ojos Calentes, depending on whether, like Pascal, you're standing on this side or that side of the Southern border.

✳

Christmas
with the People of the Promised Land

For Pierre Lazareff

This took place in 1910, on board the *Volturno*, a cargo ship that had just taken on passengers in Libya in order to transport them to New York, a full cargo of the most poverty-stricken emigrants in the world among whom I'd been taken on as an interpreter.

The *Volturno* was a very small cargo ship, not much on the transatlantic run, but a good little wooden clog that stood up well on the sea. Still, people croaked to death from the cold and from being a bit hungry, too.

It was crammed to the breaking point with the poor, the poor from every corner of the Asian countries, Siberians and Tartars, Georgians and Persians, Armenians and Kirghisians, Mohammedans from the oil countries, nomadic Buddhists from the steppes, plus a few rare Chinese from the North, some Manchurian giants, and then Jews, an abundance of poor Jews

who were coming from every ghetto in Poland and were chanting in groups on the bridge to drive away their anxiety and to proclaim their eagerness for the New World, the Promised Land....

The crossing was a long one: twenty-eight days. And that's because we were caught, just before Christmas, in an appalling storm during which the *Volturno* lost its propeller.

They had to close the portholes and seal all exits in order to safeguard the mass of people in the holds. The shuddering hull of the *Volturno* rang out with the lamentations of those wretches enclosed in the depths of the holds to whom no one paid any attention despite the redoubled banging with which they hammered against the doors of the watertight bulkheads.

Christmas we spent in Newfoundland where we had to make a long stopover at Saint John's to replace the propeller. It's one of the strangest Christmases of my life, with all those companions of misery, that miscellaneous crowd gathered in the sheds of the port inspector, each one thanking Heaven for having escaped the horrid dangers of the abyss, for having arrived in the Promised Land.

Each one honored his God and gave Him thanks in his fashion: the Parsees keeping the kitchen fires blazing in the open air by dumping in whatever glasses of brandy they were served; the Jews standing with their hats on along the corrugated-iron sides of the dock sheds, as if before the Wailing Wall, loudly sighing and crying and tearing the tops of their caftans; the great majority speechless, numb with terror, but praying: God is God.

Christmas in New York

For Paul and Christiane Gilson

One other time, the *Volturno* comes to dock at pier 289, at the far end of Brooklyn, but that was my last voyage on board. That very night, Christmas night, 1911, I throw down my bag and with a terrific sense of relief I get out of there, strolling along the piers, then crossing that enormously overpopulated agglomeration, and that night, brimming with joy, the bars all in a holiday mood, the crowds spilling out on the sidewalks, I open up a path for myself, a heavy basketful of books and manuscripts on my shoulder, advancing slowly among the barrel organs, the kermess, gangs of youngsters, some of them wearing false noses and setting off firecrackers.

Reaching the famous Brooklyn Bridge, I resolutely walk up the elevated footbridge reserved for pedestrians and with a kind of amazed joy that strongly resembles drunkenness and that increases with every step I take in the direction of New York, whose too-well-known skyline enchants me each time I see it and more particularly tonight, stretched out there before me, rolled out on the other bank of the East River, brushed with moonlight, slashed here and there with shadows and lights and, although growing taller and taking on greater thickness, more volume and scope as I get closer and closer to it at the end of the bridge, looking more and more unreal with each step I take because of its millions of illuminated windows and doors that are watching me come....I feel dizzy, my head is spinning, and for once, I feel lost.

Where do I turn? Where do I go? Which neighborhood? Which house do I choose? Which door do I open? Install myself in which window to watch, in my turn, while another arrives, the next man, lost like myself, between heaven and earth on the wild platform of that bridge?

When I reach the end of the bridge, I don't walk into New York right away but tumble down the metal spiral staircase inlaid in the right-bank abutment and I come out at water level in Chinatown, flanked with buildings big and small, all more or less ramshackle and dingy, with the exception of one structure 20 or 30 stories tall, pierced through by a hundred-odd windows before each of which flickers a Chinese lantern. There's no question of choice, I run across the embankment and make for the only house near the wharf that's lit up, push the door open, a second door, and barge into the premises.

Amazement stops me dead in my tracks. I drop my basket to the floor and stare.

I'd entered a Jewish ritual slaughterhouse. In front of me, mounted on a stack of little cages, a young rabbi was officiating, a skullcap on his head, flossy ringlets on his temples, his sleeves rolled up but the little strips of the Torah tied in knots to his elbows. His hands were bloodied, and, without letting up, he was slitting the throats of live chickens being handed to him with a single stroke of his blade curved like the knife of the sacrificer or the circumciser. It was work that called for delicacy and precision but nevertheless it was work *à l'américaine*, that is, assembly-line work, since the pullets came from the far left, where the chicken cages were piled up to the ceiling, and easily passed to the far right, where the chickens, after being plucked, disemboweled, ticketed, and packaged, moved out smartly in wheeled carts pushed into elevators that brought them to the delivery trucks that dropped them off throughout the city; and from one end of this chain to the other, the chickens passing from hand to hand were never allowed to stop except during this half or quarter second during which the rabbi's knife slit their throats with one sure stroke.

Once in a while, a recalcitrant or badly handled or bungled chicken would slip out of someone's hands and flutter away, letting fly a gurgling and deathly cackle. That didn't bother anyone since nothing could be permitted to interfere with the rhythm of the chain, whose timing made no allowances for losses. A patriarch, armed with an iron-tipped stick, would simply impale the beheaded bird and heave it in a hamper marked: FOR THE ORPHANS OF TEL-AVIV.

Christmas in Rotterdam

For Madame Antoinette Andrieux

The *Volturno* reminds me of still another maritime Christmas, in Rotterdam. Damn that ship.

I'd become friends with Peter Van der Keer, a writer on board, and when the ship made this unscheduled stopover at Rotterdam, he'd decided to drop in on his sister whom he hadn't seen in ten years. He knew she'd married a railroad man and was the mother of a family, but he no longer knew how many kids she'd had exactly.

However, since he knew very well what families were like, Peter was lugging on his back a bagful of toys bought here and there, all over the world, wherever his ship happened to stop: Japanese dolls and Mexican clay figurines; large Polynesian fetishes and African bugaboos with pieces of mirror held in their bellies; shell necklaces and glass beads; Indian birds with their dazzling tufts of ruffled feathers that you hang on an invisible thread and that seem to fly because they're so sensitive to the least little breeze; frogs from Guatemala which have a rubber band twisted into their bellies and croak and tumble over when you release them on the table; and terrific little toy trucks bought in New York for the boys.

We were having honest-to-goodness Santa Claus weather. Lots of fog. There were fantastic gusts of wind. We were coming through the heart of the Bloom district, the famous nighttown of Rotterdam, which wasn't red-hot at all, or maybe it was too early yet. The leprous houses plunged into the blackish waters of the canal and with every blast of wind, bricks came smacking to the sidewalk like soft, juicy chaws of tobacco. You could hear the convulsive wheezing of player pianos or the whooping cough spasms of pipe organs through the closed doors of the bars and the hoarse lamentations of barrel organs in the courtyards.

We finally arrived, between the dikes and the polders, at the house where my friend's sister lived. And there we fell in with the bunch of brats playing in the shed with an old soap box. How many were there? I don't know any more: six, seven, eight.... There was Jantje, the oldest, ten years old, and Sjanke, the youngest, a year old, on the lap of the oldest who was feeding him with a bottle; then the team of Zons and Peer who were twins; and also Flip, Guust, Totje, a little black snake, and I don't know who else, I forget. Anyway, the series wasn't over: my buddy's sister was expecting another brat on her little farm lost in this watery wilderness...and Peter went into his sister's room to help her, to hug her.

So I started unpacking the uncle's bag of toys: for Totje, who was howling like a little madman, the red New York fire truck with the big ladder; for Flip who was crying and Guust who was laughing, the frogs that jumped and croaked; for Peer with the big head, the masks from Africa and the birds from Guatemala; there was also a manger with its Little Jesus, from Mexico, and all its exotic little personages; and there was a boxful of pastries a little warped by the rain, with little tarts, some cream puffs, meringues, milfoils, little cakes filled with chocolate or crunched almonds, with cinnamon, with vanilla, with cream, with black cherry jam, powdered or glazed with sugar, some rum-flavored sponge cakes, some gum drops which I had brought.

The kids weren't budging. They weren't touching a thing. They'd never seen the likes of this. They didn't know what these things were. All these toys spread out in front of them stunned them, indeed, flabbergasted them, and all these cakes— they didn't know if they could be eaten. Suddenly, one of them starts crying, the others start howling, and in no time the whole house is filled with sharp screams, curses, groans, plaintive cries, as if a pig were being bled in the kitchen.

I saw Peter running out, telling me: "Let's get the fuck out, it's my sister who's in labor.... It's terrible, unbelievable, you've no idea..." He was furious. We ran like a couple of thieves. The floodgates of heaven were open, a lukewarm rain was pouring, strange, brackish, containing bits of herring scales, as if it were being dumped out of brining barrels.

It all ended at *The Midnight Tango* in the most unbeliev- able brawl I ever took part in in my life, and I'll never forget what a ruckus, what a lunatic music a piano can make when it shatters against the ground after falling from the third floor. A thousand tomcats meowing in the night, a thousand she-cats in heat....

✳

Christmas in Bahía

For Maria Frias

In Bahía, the Rome of the Blacks of Brazil, in Bahía-de-todos-los-Santos, the Bay-of-all-the-Saints where there are more churches than days of the year, in Bahía, at the Church of Bom-Fim, of the Good Death, which is the parish of the Negroes, they celebrate, on the feast of the Nativity, the Mass of the Cock, and the crowd of the faithful that presses around the manger adores not so much the Divine Child as the one among the three kings who was a Black: it celebrates the idea that Gaspar and his big elephant come out of Africa, out of the kingdom of the Queen of Sheba, were able to get to paradise and throw open the doors of heaven not only to the Black Africans but also to their animals....

That's the reason why, in the mangers of Bahía, the bull and the donkey are often a camel and a water buffalo, and a procession of domestic and indigenous animals surround them with all the wild animals of the Ancient and New Worlds, to lean over the Little Child, who is often a little Negro and more often still a little Negress that wiggles in the straw at the far end of the overcrowded church. And then there is the cock....

As with the Greeks, the cock of Asklepios,[9] the cock of the backyard—his song, his slaughtering, the squirting of his blood—occupy an important place in Negro witchcraft. Thus, he figures in the manger. His sacrifice is still a tradition. I've seen, in a manger in Bahía, a living cock take the place of the star of Bethlehem. In another church, a dead cock was driven into the star with a long arrow, and in the Chapel of Bom-Fim a black cock was impaled on a golden sword from which gushed out, zigzagging in an orange sky, three lightning bolts bearing in letters of tar the name of Herod....

But the Mass of the Cock is not a tragedy. It's a celebration of the joy of living, of being in this world, and the animals of Creation, like in the legends of Africa, play a primary role in it. To the point where even in the middle of prayers and hymns, the attendants imitate the cries of animals, some trumpet, others bellow, bleat, howl, bark, yelp, whistle, coo, and let out resounding cock-a doodle-dos that chime in every corner, while at the church door the beggars sing out:

> *Viva, viva, viva,*
> *Viva a alegría*
> *Na casa de Voss' Senhoría!*

Christmas in the Foreign Legion

*In memory of Dame Peluche's
cacklings*

When Corporal Oliver Sullivan came to, he saw the sun as if through a reddish mist. He had fallen backwards, his head down at the bottom of a shell hole, his two feet over the edge. Some barbed wire was slicing at his neck.

He made an effort, pulled in his feet, and managed to crouch in the bottom of the hole. Just then a flow of blood spurted into his face. He noticed he no longer had a nose and had just vomited his tongue. He tried to stand up but was immediately greeted by a volley of German grenades. So he quickly hit the dirt, taking cover behind the bodies of his two buddies killed right next to him.

After that, he wasn't budging.

The morning was passing. The sun was climbing in the sky, was tumbling into his lacerated mouth, seemed to want to pull out his tonsils. Corporal Sullivan had gone blind.

Suddenly, he heard some German voices less than twenty feet away. He remembered his orders. He was supposed to pick off a German sentry. He had set out at night with the Spaniard, Aymerol, and Khabok, the Czech poet. A grenade had laid them out in here, a few feet away from their goal. The captain had told them: "Go pick off a German sentry for me as a Christmas present and you get a furlough in Paris."

Pick off....

It was noon. Corporal Oliver Sullivan could hear the Germans come and go in their trench. They were calling out to each other. Someone had just brought them some soup. In a flash, Corporal Sullivan was standing on the edge of the German trench with a grenade in each hand. He was a fright to look at, having no face left and his dangling jaw hooked onto his ears. He couldn't shout, but blood flowed in little clots from his open gash. He threw his first grenade in the midst of the Fritzies about to break bread. Those who escaped didn't wait for what would come next. They jumped out of the trench, obeying blind instinct, and went scattering quickly across the 500-odd feet that separated them from the French trench. There were five.

Corporal Oliver Sullivan was right behind them. His laughter was a gurgling of blood. He fell, clumsily, to the bottom of the trench. It was his five Kraut prisoners who buried him.

Christmas in the Ardennes Forest

For Roger and Nadine Nimier

I'd reserved my table by telephone and I was eager to get to Paris for the *réveillon*.[10] It was already well onto five o'clock in the afternoon, night was approaching, and the dense drizzle that was falling turned to ice as soon as it touched the pavement. My car was in front of the door. Roux, the gamekeeper, grumblingly threw in a hamper of game, then went out to fetch a young fir tree which I wanted to bring along to give a note of gaiety, an atmosphere of innocence to my reserved table at the *Boeuf sur le Toit*.[11] Since he was going about it all wrong and was putting no good will into it, I had to give him a hand to place the tree in the car, then I plopped myself behind the wheel.

"It bothers me to see you leave without having fired a shot," said Roux.

"It doesn't make the least bit of difference, *mon vieux*. I prefer to leave a little early. In this kind of weather, this fog and iciness on the roads, I won't be setting any records. I'll be lucky if I get there on time. I'll send you a post card and a jar of Ambrine[12] for your nose! Have I forgotten anything...?"

Roux was in a bad mood. He walked away without saying a word and came back out of his shed holding a rabbit by the ears which he threw from a distance into the car, went into his barn and returned with a flask and two glasses in his hands:

"Bottoms up," he said.

"Bottoms up," I said.

And I burst out laughing, because he looked so funny with his ruddy snout that seemed about to drop off like a rotten banana.

"Take care of your nose," I told him. "You'll end up losing it without even noticing. It's frozen to the roots!"

Impossible to cheer him up. Roux was in a terrible mood. And he was in a terrible mood because he wasn't very proud of himself. And now he was furious.

He'd been in a terrible mood for eight days, because for eight days he'd dragged me over hills and across valleys through the woods in some very fresh wild boar tracks without succeeding in tracking down any prey; he wasn't proud of himself because of eight consecutive days spent lying in wait for an old solitary which he never stopped talking about, a *bête noire* if there ever was one, "as big as an ox," he insisted, "and so much heavier from all the lead I've shot point-blank into his belly that there's no trace of hair left on his backbone." Still we came back each time empty-handed, without even having seen a cub; and now he was angry because I was talking about his nose, a fine naked bird but all lit up, running, as ruddy and purple as an eggplant, soft and swollen in an uncouth and stupid way since the previous night when, in the depths of a thicket, not moving a muscle, lying in wait for the beast that wouldn't come, Roux had fallen asleep and come down with frostbite.

"Well, aren't you going to let me have a box of your famous shoeshine?" I asked the gamekeeper, a foot on the starter and ready to get going.

There are days when you make nothing but mistakes. In fact, the story of the shoeshine which Roux claimed he'd invented was a subject even more likely to get him angry than a simple reference to the misfortune which had befallen his nasal appendix. In his more confiding moments, Roux would readily tell you he had this wonderful shoeshine which, when applied to his boots, attracted rabbits which would immediately start following him, and that often he'd walked into his own kitchen with 25 or 30 rabbits docile to the point of allowing themselves to be picked right up. Naturally, they didn't jump into the saucepan to be stewed of their own accord or under the chopping-knife to be cut up into tidbits, naturally not, but Roux got all riled up and would start cussing up and down if you didn't believe his story.

"What the devil! Why on earth do you need my shoeshine since you're heading for Paris!" he shouted, and the keeper disappeared into his cabin and slammed the door.

"So long! See you again!" I bellowed out.

And I zoomed off blowing my horn at him once, ten times, a hundred times. The woods filled up with the sound of me.

Sure, I needed his shoeshine.

I thought about it a hundred times, a thousand times, on the road, and every now and then I'd slow down to see if the rabbits were following me. What a treat it would have been, on Christmas night, to smear my tires with old man Roux' Miracle Shoeshine and to have all the rabbits of the Northern plains in my wake, galloping along behind the car, from the Ardennes to the Place de la Concorde, and to kick open the door to the bar, leaping into the *Boeuf sur le Toit* to the consternation of the guests—all those beautiful ladies bedecked with pearl necklaces, all the young people, the esthetes, and the Negro jazz band....

I walked in there roaring with laughter.

"What's the matter?" people kept asking me. "You been drinking...?"

✳

Christmas at the Boeuf sur le Toit

For Coco Chanel

At those all-night parties at the *Boeuf*, during the great era of Moysès, when Clément Doucet and Jean Wiener were always playing their duo pianos without end—as soon as I walked in, I knew who I'd find there. There was the dowager, the old Duchess d'Uzès, dressed up like a sailor, with her straight talk, her cutty pipe, her bottle of bordeaux. There was Coco Chanel, the loner. When the jazz band struck up, Jean Cocteau, like a will o' the wisp, his fuse smelling out the heat, would move up closer to the fire. There was Marthe Chenal who was trying one more time to get her grappling-irons into that white nigger, Ambroise Vollard, by making him dance. There was Peignot the publisher who, on leaving the *Boeuf* one Christmas night, had driven his car down the entrance of the *métro de la Madeleine* and had managed to drive it right back out, rear-end forwards. There was Madame Leygues and her famous necklace with the I-no-longer-remember-how-many-yards of pearls, Misia Sert, the young composer Georges Auric, and old Fargue....

Fargue, Ravel, Vollard, Misia, the Duchess d'Uzès, Madame Leygues, Marthe Chenal—

> *Tell me where, in what country,*
> *Is Flora, the comely Roman....?*
> *Or Archipiada, or Thaïs....?*
> *Where is the learnèd Heloïse....?*
> *Queen Blanche as white as a lily....?*
> *Bertha of the big feet, Beatrice, Alice,*
> *And the worthy Joan of Lorraine*
> *Whom the English burnt at Rouen?*
> *O where are the snows of long, long ago?*

Christmas in Rio

For Madame Simone

Y ou no sooner say Christmas than it's here!

You've got to revise even your most time-honored poetic ideas.

Here in Rio, Christmas falls at the height of the austral summer, and the mere fact of existing is sheer happiness.

It's in Rio that I learned how to be leery of logic.

Living is a magical act.

"Is the eye to the left or the right of the hand?" asks an old Negro proverb.

That's no enigma. It's a wizard's recipe in the form of a riddle, and you've got to answer: "It's a butterfly!"

It's a game.

It teaches you how to see better and to penetrate the mysterious essence of things.

A butterfly!

It's an idea, an idea that suddenly came into your head and that you allowed to fly around while shaking your head the way you do when one of those marvelous tropical butterflies that come out of the adjacent virgin forests loses its way and comes fluttering around your outlandish skull as if it were the rarest of flowers in this exotic roof-garden suspended at the top of the Hotel Gloria.

The wonderful giant lepidoptera, which is as large as a man's hand and has blue wings bordered with black, tries to alight, but his insistence makes you uneasy after a while and you wind up chasing him away with loud strokes of your towel, and the far-flying creature, possibly voracious, capsizes overboard and falls into an abyss of heat, perplexed, tipsy with sunshine and light, flies in a heavy and irregular fashion as if bent on losing itself in the dim blue, is seemingly borne away, I won't say

> Helter-skelter,
> Like a
> Falling leaf

because in Brazil the leaves aren't deciduous, but like a soul in trouble and tired of drifting.

Even among the peoples of remotest antiquity, the butterfly was an emblem of reincarnation and was considered the herald angel of a death near at hand, meaning a FRESH START.

At any rate, here it's summer.

Christmas.

1

One person who believed in reincarnation, but who couldn't accept the belief that death was a necessary and unavoidable prelude to the transmigration of souls because she had escaped it once already, was a paralytic, a Russian, the Countess Starotsa, a madwoman, an *illuminée*, miraculously rescued from the shipwreck of the *Principessa Mafalda* and living for the past twenty-five years on the top floor, right under the hanging gardens of the Hotel Gloria, in an apartment whose windows all look out over Rio, its incomparable bay, the mountains opposite, the burnished brow of the light of the first morning of Creation like the mountains that serve as geological backdrops in the paintings of Leonardo or Mantegna, the sudsy ocean, the islands, the peaks, the crags, the pyramid of Sugarloaf, the dreary neighbors, the agaves, the palm trees, and the disquieting forest from which come the butterflies.

"I don't want to die," she kept saying. "All souls are inside us. All we have to do is choose the one we want to be. It's an act of will power. No one dies. No one is reincarnated. We just barely change skins! But it's still a miracle. I willed it in the name of the Holy Ghost. Look at me, I've already undergone a first metamorphosis and I didn't die of it. But I insist on a second miracle because I want to heal. I pray. I concentrate. I totally focus myself. I call on the Holy Ghost. On board the *Principessa Mafalda* it happened by itself, instantaneously. These days, it's harder. I'm too often distracted from my exercises and dragged out of my yoga by the planes that fly beneath my windows. There are too many. It's the work of the devil. Where do they come from? Where are they going? It doesn't get you anywhere. I want to live. A poor caterpillar turns into a resplendent butterfly. Look here, look at my collection."

And she'd point to her collection of the most beautiful butterflies of Brazil pinned to the walls inside massive mahogany cases.

She herself was without a doubt the most staggering item in her collection, a kind of spectral butterfly caught in a net, stretched out as she was in her hammock before the open window of her grand drawing-room, her black silhouette—half-stiff, half-living—the legs all withered away, the breasts sagging, coming apart at the brink of the luminous abyss at the bottom of which Rio languishes during the day, its abstract skyscrapers seeping out of the vaporish heat, and out of which climbs the night with its electric streetlights that go on all at once and the constellations that rise one after another out of the sea, the Southern Cross, the full moon, the muffled but grumbling tom-tom of the *macoumbas* celebrated by Black sorcerers all over the surrounding hillsides.

Then she'd call for candles of black wax which gave off an odor of incense while burning, and she'd gulp down a drug that had the consistency of honey and swallow a huge glassful of some boiling potion.

"It's to protect me from the cold, I'm cold!" she'd say in her Slavic accent which put an impassioned cooing in her throat. "I have faith in the miracle! Look at me, I'm like a larva midway to the resurrection, a chrysalid. Already, I can never die. I see the Holy Ghost...."

She was probably an adventuress and she must have been making converts because every night hundreds of people would go up to her place and there were high times in her drawing-room. Somebody had to pay the hotel bills of the miraculous countess! What the hell, life's expensive in Rio.

2

And here's what had happened to her at the time of the *Principessa Mafalda* shipwreck in 1927:

The transatlantic steamer had just circled the Cape and already the signal was being briskly given from the bridge for the debarkation. The hatches were open. They were hoisting the glamorous new automobiles from the holds, removing all the rigging to make sure they'd be ready to roll quickly. They were getting the baggage of the first-class passengers together on the deck, giving them numbers for the customs officials. The families were gathered in the ship's lounges, the children dressed, the mothers all properly decked out, the maids supervising the hand baggage, the nannies caressing the little treasures that had been entrusted to them, the daddies checking their wallets one last time to make sure they had all their documents in order: passport, debarkation forms, declarations. Others were paying their bill, handing out tips to the service personnel, cabin-boys, officious maîtres d's, waiters. A few couples were dancing at the bar. They were drinking champagne. Taking a break.

The ship's orchestra was playing a last tango when someone signaled the bridge that the turbines had been damaged. There was an absolute calm. The weather was radiant. It was between ten and eleven in the morning. They were no more than twelve, maybe fifteen miles from Rio de Janeiro. The coast was in sight. They were surrounded by ten or twelve ships all heading for the harbor, coming from all points of the compass. The captain refused to believe danger was impending. One of the turbines was still running. They'd get in late of course and that was annoying, but he was convinced he'd be able to steer his fine ship into port and not botch its arrival, without fanfare but without having had to ask for anyone's help, a matter of great pride to a sailor. And then catastrophe struck. Suddenly, cataracts of water crashed into the holds, flooded the boilers, and the whole vessel keeled over dangerously. And there was panic—a panic that lasted until five in the afternoon, rising to a crescendo, surpassing all the bounds of crime and of horror as long as the ship remained afloat and until it foundered by flip-flopping over and slithering stern-downwards into the abyss. Because of a stupid stubbornness that beclouded his mind, the captain hadn't sent out an SOS to the port authorities so close by, not even a wireless to the company's general agent to ask for the help of a tugboat, just as he'd refused until the last minute all offers of help that had been made by the ships that surrounded him and had imperceptibly approached his own, remaining all day long in his vicinity, ready to intervene.

At the end of the tragedy, when they were finally able to put out their lifeboats, it was too late. Those passengers who hadn't been murdered were being mutilated by the stampeding deckhands crazy with terror—a crew of Sidis and Lascars, hired for a pittance in the wake of a strike, who had been pillaging the baggage, cutting off fingers and ears, strangling and eviscerating in order to steal the jewelry the women wore around their necks or the money they'd been able to conceal in their money-belts. Those who jumped overboard were being devoured by sharks. The face of the sea was ruddy with blood.

There were hundreds of deaths and a handful of rescues, a lifeboat or two, among whom was the Countess Starosta. From the onset of panic, she had backed up against the mainmast, her two arms clasped behind her, face to face with danger, breasts held high, eyes fixed to a spot in the sky, seeing nothing of the horrors taking place around her, spouting her act of faith like a challenge: *"In the name of the Holy Ghost, may the Father and the Son perform a miracle of Life!"*

And she had felt a blow to her stomach and when they'd pulled her out of the water, both her legs were paralyzed, from the hips to the ankles, from the heels to the very tips of her toes. The psychiatrists attributed her paralysis to a cerebral stroke, but the Countess wouldn't hear of it: "It's the cold that caught hold of me," she explained. "I'm a Russian. I know all about the evil doings of the cold. I don't want to go back to my native country. Let me live here. I want to heal. And someday I'll return to Heaven, which is my real country. It will be a second prodigy. I do everything to instigate it. I wish it...."

3

A while ago I received an airmail letter informing me of the death of the Countess Starosta in Rio. According to what they tell me, she didn't die in the odor of sanctity, despite her efforts, her faith, and what she'd believed she was or would become.

> *...It was Christmas Day. She was stretched out in her hammock hanging before that corner window which you know very well, the one from which one is tempted to jump in order to leap straight from the Gloria into paradise. You can rest assured our dear Countess didn't commit suicide. But things weren't going well at all, and she could feel herself getting weaker. At a given moment she bared her belly, exposing it fully to the light, and murmured almost inaudibly: "In the name of the Holy Ghost, may the Sunlight make me melt! I feel ice-cold.... Look.... I'm flying off...!" Everybody had his eyes fastened to the open window; if the poor thing had had a soul, even as fragile and transparent as a snowflake from her native country, everybody would have seen it pass or fall into the void or ascend into heaven, because all of us were expecting a miracle ever since she had managed to bewitch us. But the sky remained desperately empty. There wasn't a flicker of a shadow, not even a semblance. Not so much as a gnat's wing flitted in the abyss, let alone a hummingbird's. Not a butterfly missing from the cases. It was quite plain to everybody. There were more than thirty witnesses, including my brother Oswaldo and me—*

> *Yan*

4

A nother year, another woman came to disturb the sybaritic habits of the permanent residents at the Hotel Gloria.

She was a certain Baronesse de la Verrière, who was said to be the wife of the richest banker in Vienna.

She was an extremely tall blonde, very thin and very given to chills, whose doctor had ordered her to go spend Christmas in Rio de Janeiro in order to get warmed up.

From the night of her arrival, the lady had caused a revolution at the hotel by ordering that the ventilators be turned off, that the windows in the mezzanine be closed, that electric radiators be installed in every corner of the bar, that folding-screens be placed around the table where she sat, with a comforter, smothered in furs, her feet on a heater, screeching like a hysterical parakeet whenever anyone presumed to leave a door open, calling for sweaters and blankets every time she changed tables or corners, grating on the nerves of the bridge- and canasta-players who weren't uttering a peep, too polite to protest but consigning that woman to the depths of hell, sweating, melting, soaking in their heavily starched white tuxedos, dabbing their foreheads, fanning themselves with their playing cards, the counters sticking to their fingers.

They had nicknamed the creature "Venus in Furs," and luckily the neuropath decamped before the week was over, just before Christmas Eve, after receiving a cable from her doctor recommending that she go to Djibouti, which his inquiries revealed was the warmest spot on the planet.... And it was only then that they found out that the self-effacing man who traveled with her, who never said a word, who waited patiently in a chair, his arms loaded with kerchiefs and woolens and plaids and blankets and coats, who on a whim of his compan- ion would fall on his knees to help her with her fur-lined boots, was none other than the famous A.J. Mayer, king of the investors on the Stock Exchange, one of the fiercest sharks in international finance. Everyone had taken him for the eccen- tric lady's chauffeur.

5

Is the eye to the right or the left of the hand?

To the memory of Sam Putnam

Is the eye to the right or the left of the hand?" asks an old Negro proverb.

It's the lens I use to size things up in Brazil, because you've got to have a bit of magic.

For example:

Here in Rio the leaves aren't deciduous and Christmas falls at the height of austral summer.

"Have you noticed, Cendrars, that the skyscrapers here have no chimneys?" I was asked by Samuel Putnam,[13] a university professor from Chicago who has come over to get a bird's-eye view of Brazilian Literature in order to situate it with greater precision in the panorama of the literary history of the three Americas, "and that this absence of chimneys disturbs and disorients one...."

It was a pertinent remark. We were drinking whiskey in the roof-garden of the Hotel Gloria (*Gloria in excelsis!* I kept saying while guzzling, I was so happy to be in Rio for Christmas once again) and from that high up, we overlooked the roofs of the entire modern metropolis. Sure enough, not a single chimney defiled the countryside around the Bay of Guanabarà, which reflected the blue immensities of its sky and its luminous mountains, and unlike those of New York and Chicago, not one of the skyscrapers of Rio de Janeiro was wreathed with clouds of soot or endless swirls of smog. The city was simply there—a proud capital, an abstract design.

"So then, what do you conclude?" I asked Sam.

"I don't know," he answered. "Must I conclude that Taine's theory to the effect that the influence of décor, of setting, of Nature, of geographical ambience on the national literature of a people is false or out of date, or must I consider the lack of a specifically Brazilian philosophy in the phenomenon of this country's literary production to be a side-effect of climate? The Brazilian doesn't need artificial heat. He doesn't meditate by the fire. He takes siestas. Which explains his credulity, his lack of resourcefulness, his visions, his infantilism, etc., etc."

All of this explained nothing at all, and I had a hard time following the reasoning or my friend, a typical scholar from the U.S.A., hung up on logic. Since we were nearing Christmas, his original observations made me think of the kids of Rio—the kids of the rich who aren't able to hang up their stockings by the chimney since there aren't any chimneys in the residential skyscrapers along the shoreline—the kids of the poor, those of the near and the distant coastal suburbs, as well as those of the *favelas,* those savage places at the very heart of the city, which have fire, you bet, a primeval fire which smoulders beneath the ashes of the most miserable hovels, at the dreary center of the capital as well as at the dreary limits of the hinterland—I was thinking of the poor who have fire in the house but can't hang their stockings by the chimney because they haven't got any stockings....

The Problem of Heating doesn't, therefore, present itself. Everybody goes barefoot. Everybody's quite content.

You no sooner say Christmas than it's here!

And in Rio, it comes at the heart of summer.

*

*   *

Sam died the other year without concluding, but there was something to his still-unpublished thesis. What? I don't know, for sure. An idea....

But one doesn't get the idea to come to Rio to expound ideas. It's so good, over here, just to be alive. The mere fact of existing is sheer happiness.... Ever since, I've been leery of logic.

(Christmas, 1953)

✱

Notes: Biographical and Critical

Christmas in New Zealand

[1] "land of Heart's Desire": The phrase in Cendrars' original text, *pays du Tendre*, is rather difficult to translate into English. This "land of Tenderness" (literally) is an imaginary country, complete with map and sundry specifics about adjacent areas, invented by the *précieuse* French novelist, Mademoiselle de Scudéry (1607–1701). Readers of her interminable novels are instructed in the amatory arts and in the diverse modes of approach (platonic, sentimental, anatomical) which one may adopt to reach one's goal. There are many levels of initiation and many stages along the way. But for true lovers, the ultimate bliss is attained only when they reach the *pays du Tendre* proper.

[2] "Southern Cross": Constellation visible solely in the skies of the southern hemisphere. It is in the shape of a cross and its vertical axis points towards the South Pole. (Notice Cendrars' allusion to "gigantic crucifix-shaped ferns" a little earlier.)

[3] *"Pagliacci"*: Presumably a piano transcription of the opera *I Pagliacci* by the Italian composer Ruggiero Leoncavallo (1858–1919).

[4] "An Anzac from Artois": *Anzac* is an acronym for the Australian and New Zealand Army Corps, a name given to the "Kangaroo" Australian troops stationed in Egypt during World War I. The Anzacs were heroic in the catastrophic battle at Gallipoli. After regrouping in Egypt, the Anzac division took part in the first battle of the Somme, then notably Messines, third battle of Ypres, Passchendaele, Beaucourt, Bapaume and Le Quesney. This, I would suggest, is the "Artois" connection, Artois being the French province located between the Parisian basin and the plains of Flanders where bloody battles of the Great War took place. The plum pudding and whiskey suggest a British rather than a French tradition.

Christmas and New Year's Day in China

[5] "General Ma": Chung-li Ma (1885–1944), Chinese military man who first served the cause of Nationalist leader Chiang Kai-shek but later

switched his allegiance to the guerilla forces of Mao Tse-tung. Notorious for the ferocity of his tactics, he was executed by the Japanese before the end of World War Two.

[6] "Jules Janin":   Jules Janin (1804–1874), French drama critic, known chiefly for his acerbic essays in the Paris periodical *Journal des débats*. Elected to the Académie française in 1865. *The Dead Donkey and the Guillotined Woman,* Janin's only novel, is now completely forgotten and Cendrars is clearly making use of it for the suggestiveness of its gory title.

Christmas with Max Jacob

[7] "Max Jacob":   Max Jacob (1876–1944), French poet of Jewish descent, close friend of Picasso, Erik Satie, Guillaume Apollinaire, and Jean Cocteau, converted to Catholicism in 1909 after a rapturous mystical experience, and thereafter author of dazzling and whimsically devout poems and prose. He claimed to have frequent visions of the Blessed Virgin Mary and favorite saints, and to chat with them. He lived in such intense poverty that he buttoned his overcoat to the neck, even in summer, to conceal his nakedness. The Nazis put an end to his miseries in a concentration camp in 1944.

[8] "rue Gabrielle":   Grubby little cul-de-sac in Paris, near Montmartre, where Max Jacob lived and held court for his young followers and artist-friends in the early years of the century. Similar to Gertrude Stein's rue de Fleurus a few years later.

Christmas in Bahía

[9] "Asklepios":   Revered by the Ancient Greeks as the founder of Medicine, Asklepios learned the arts of healing both from Apollo and from Cheiron and established a famous semi-occult healing center at Epidaurus. With the use of the Gorgon Medusa's blood given to him by Athena, he had the power to raise the dead. His followers later substituted cock's blood for Gorgon-blood. According to Sir James Frazer (cf. *The Golden Bough*), Asklepios' name means "mistletoe" and it was with mistletoe in hand that Aeneas (a devotee of the Asklepian magical cult) visited the Underworld and it was through its thaumaturgic power that he was allowed to return at will to "the upper air."

Christmas in the Ardennes Forest

[10] *"réveillon"*:   A uniquely French, all-night holiday party of sustained eating and drinking which traditionally takes place at Christmas and New Year's. The name of the custom suggests that those who binge on these occasions remain awake until dawn.

[11] *"Boeuf sur le Toit"*:   Originally the title of a theatrical farce by Jean Cocteau, Darius Milhaud, and Léonide Massine, produced by the brothers Fratellini at the *Comédie des Champs-Elysées* in 1920. The following year, *Le Boeuf sur le Toit (The Bull on the Rooftop)* became the name of a cabaret-bar presided over by Jean Cocteau which soon became a favorite hang-out for the French and international artistic and literary Bohemia of the *entre deux guerres.* Some of its famous and near-famous patrons included the young Picasso and Modigliani as well as Clément Doucet (1883–1936) and Jean Wiener (1888–1948), popular composers, vaudeville artists, and pianists who flourished at that period; the Duchess d'Uzès (1871–1933), an eccentric aristocrat, transvestite, and patroness of avant-garde artists; Louis Moysès (1878–1949), the witty French impresario and theater director; Coco Chanel (1899–1959), patroness of the arts and heiress to the Chanel perfume fortune; Jean Cocteau (1889–1963), poet and cinéaste (*Le Sang d'un Poète, Orphée, La Belle et la Bête*); Marthe Chenal (1899–1942), amateur painter and cabaret dancer; Ambroise Vollard (1868–1939), publisher and art dealer who was the first to make known the works of Gauguin and Cézanne; Achille-Louis Peignot (1879–1930), patron of the arts, *bon vivant,* and publisher of bibelots and avant-garde limited editions; Madame Pérégrine Leygues (1877–1950), wife of a millionaire Paris art collector and amateur aviator, Georges Leygues; Misia Sert (1891–1938), cabaret dancer and singer; Georges Auric (1899–1983), French composer, member of the famous musical group christened "les Six" by Jean Cocteau which also included Darius Milhaud, Arthur Honegger, Germaine Tailleferre, Francis Poulenc, and Louis Durey—Auric wrote the musical scores to films ranging from Cocteau's *Orphée* and *La Belle et la Bête* in the 1930s to John Huston's *Moulin Rouge* in 1952; Léon-Paul Fargue (1876–1947), French poet and memoirist known chiefly for his lyrical evocations of Paris street life, *Le Piéton de Paris* (1939); Maurice Ravel (1875–1937), French composer famous especially for his ballets *Daphnis and Chloé* (1912), *La Valse* (1920), and Boléro (1928). The Nazis ordered the famous cabaret closed in 1943, but it was at a reopened *Le Boeuf sur le Toit* that the youthful Juliette Gréco (1927–   ) was first introduced to the Paris public in the late 1940s.

[12] "jar of Ambrine":   French pharmaceutical product current in the 1930s and 1940s. An amber-colored mixture of paraffin and resin somewhat thicker than Vick's Vaporub and with a strong resinous smell, it was used chiefly to heal burns and chilblains (frostbite).

Christmas in Rio

[13] "Samuel Putnam":   Samuel Putnam (1892–1950) was not only "a university professor from Chicago" and "a typical *scholar* from the U. S. A." (in Cendrars' words) but also the distinguished American translator of some 35 works from the French, Spanish, and Italian which included classic American versions of Cervantes' *Don Quixote* and of Rabelais' *Gargantua and Pantagruel.* In the 1940s, he taught in various universities in Brazil and wrote extensively on Brazilian life and literature. His memoir of expatriate life in Paris in the 1930s, *Paris Was Our Mistress* (1947), is now considered a minor classic. In this book, Putnam mentions his encounters with Cendrars in Paris and alludes to Cendrars' friendship with the American novelist John Dos Passos. It was, in fact, Dos Passos who was the first American ever to translate a text by Cendrars into English—the long poem, *Panama, or The Adventures of My Seven Uncles*—as early as 1925. In a book entitled *Orient-Express* published in 1927, Dos Passos devotes a whole chapter to the globetrotting Cendrars, whom he calls "the Homer of the Trans-Siberian."

Photo courtesy of Miriam Cendrars

About the Author

Born Frédéric-Louis Sauser in 1887 in Switzerland, Blaise Cendrars was educated in Naples, Italy, held an apprenticeship to a clockmaker in St. Petersburg, Russia, and befriended Marc Chagall, Max Jacob, Jean Cocteau and Apollinaire. His stories, plays, novels and poems earned him an international reputation and, ultimately, one of France's highest literary honors—Prix Litteraire de la Ville de Paris. Cendrars was arguably the prime catalyst of the Modernist Movement, rather than Apollinaire. Novelist John Dos Passos called Cendrars, "the Homer of the Trans-Siberian"—the railroad that connects Eastern Europe to China which Cendrars rode as a youth. He died in 1961 at the age of 73.

Georges-Antonie Diepdalle

About the Translator

Born in Lewiston, Maine, in 1936, Bertrand Mathieu has taught American literature in the U.S., France, Germany, the People's Republic of China, and the Kingdom of Saudi Arabia. He has been twice Fulbright Professor of American Literature, the first time at the University of Athens, Greece, from 1979 to 1981, and more recently at the University of Dakar, Senegal, in West Africa, from 1986 to 1987.

Mathieu has lived and traveled widely in Germany, Italy, Yugoslavia, Greece, Mexico, Turkey, Hong Kong, Taiwan, and the American Southwest, where he earned a Ph.D. in English at the University of Arizona (Tucson) in 1975. His poems, translations, reviews, and critical essays have appeared in *American Poetry Revtew, City Lights Anthology, Essays in Arts and Sciences, Chicago Review, Concerning Poetry, Partisan Review, Poetry, The Village Voice, Temenos* (London), *L'Arc* (France), and *The Southeastern Review* (Athens), of which he has been Editor-at-Large. A former Woodrow Wilson Fellow, Mathieu has been the recipient of grants from the National Endowment for the Humanities and the Lilly Foundation at Yale University.

Mathieu's book publications include a volume of poems, *Landscape with Voices* (Delta, 1965), early versions of the Rimbaud masterpieces, *A Season in Hell* (Pomegranate Press, 1977) and *A Season in Hell & Illuminations* (BOA Editions, 1991), and a mythoanalytical study of Orphism, Rimbaud, and Henry Miller entitled *Orpheus in Brooklyn*. Bertrand Mathieu currently lives in Rimbaud's native Charleville, in the French Ardennes, where he is completing a novel about his experiences in Greece, *Freeing Eurydice.*

BOA EDITIONS, LTD.
AMERICAN READER SERIES